POEMS CHOSEN BY

STARLIGHT
STARBRIGHT

Illustrated by Jane Browne

Julia MacRae Books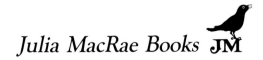

LONDON SYDNEY AUCKLAND JOHANNESBURG

FOR AMELIA   A.H.

First published 1995

1 3 5 7 9 10 8 6 4 2

Copyright in this collection © 1995 Anne Harvey
Illustrations © 1995 Jane Browne
The Acknowledgements on page 46 constitute an extension
of this copyright notice

Anne Harvey and Jane Browne have asserted their
right under the Copyright, Designs and Patents Act, 1988
to be identified as the author and illustrator of this work

First published in Great Britain 1995
by Julia MacRae
an imprint of Random House
20 Vauxhall Bridge Road, London SW1V 2SA

Random House Australia (Pty) Ltd
20 Alfred Street, Milsons Point, Sydney, NSW 2061, Australia

Random House New Zealand Ltd
18 Poland Road, Glenfield, Auckland, New Zealand

Random House South Africa (Pty) Ltd
PO Box 337, Bergvlei 2012, South Africa

Random House UK Limited Reg. No. 954009

A CIP catalogue record for this book is
available from the British Library

ISBN 1 85681 523 4 (PB)
ISBN 1 85681 097 6 (HB)

Typeset by SX Composing Ltd, Rayleigh, Essex

Printed and bound in Hong Kong

CONTENTS

Star light, star bright,
First star I see tonight,
I wish I may, I wish I might,
Have the wish I wish tonight.

Traditional

TIME TO GO HOME

Time to go home!
    Says the great steeple clock.
Time to go home!
    Says the gold weathercock.
Down sinks the sun
    In the valley to sleep;
Lost are the orchards
    In blue shadows deep.
Soft falls the dew
    On cornfield and grass;
Through the dark trees
    The evening airs pass:
Time to go home,
    They murmur and say;
Birds to their homes
    Have all flown away.
Nothing shines now
    But the gold weathercock.
Time to go home!
    Says the great steeple clock.

James Reeves

5

BEDTIME

Five minutes, five minutes more, please!
  Let me stay five minutes more!
Can't I just finish the castle
  I'm building here on the floor?
Can't I just finish the story
  I'm reading here in my book?
Can't I just finish this bead-chain —
  It *almost* is finished, look!
Can't I just finish this game, please?
  When a game's once begun
It's a pity never to find out
  Whether you've lost or won.
Can't I just stay five minutes?
  Well, can't I stay just four?
Three minutes, then? two minutes?
  Can't I stay *one* minute more?

Eleanor Farjeon

BED IN SUMMER

In winter I get up at night
And dress by yellow candle-light.
In summer, quite the other way,
I have to go to bed by day.

I have to go to bed and see
The birds still hopping on the tree,
Or hear the grown-up people's feet
Still going past me in the street.

And does it not seem hard to you,
When all the sky is clear and blue,
And I should like so much to play,
To have to go to bed by day?

Robert Louis Stevenson

GRANNY'S GONE TO SLEEP

Granny's gone to sleep:
Softly, little boys;
Read your pretty books,
Don't make a noise,
Pussy's on the stool,
Quiet as a mouse;
Not a whisper runs
Through the whole house.
Hush! silence keep;
Granny's gone to sleep.

Matthias Barr

Go to bed late,
Stay very small;
Go to bed early,
Grow very tall.

Anon

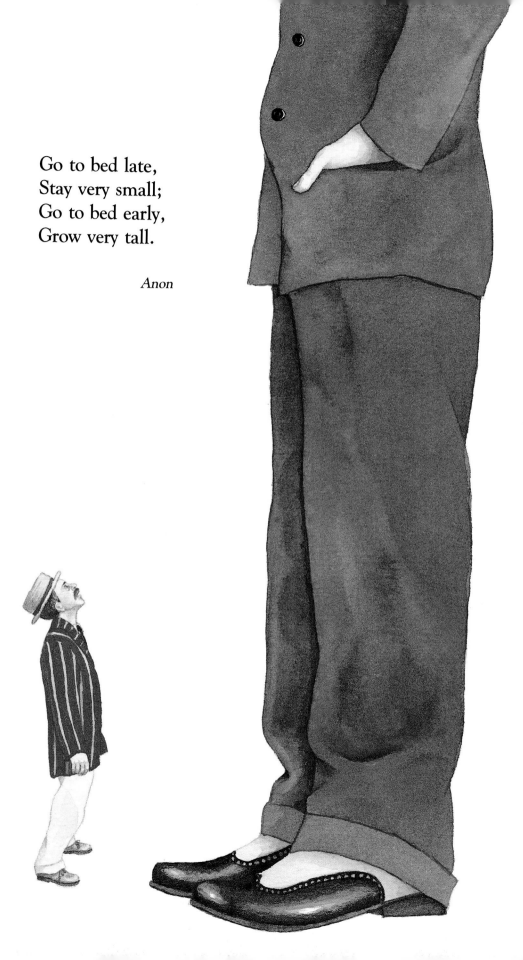

TOMMY

Young Tommy would not go to bed,
But sat watching TV instead,
   As he stayed up to stare
   His face went all square
And aerials grew from his head.

Anon

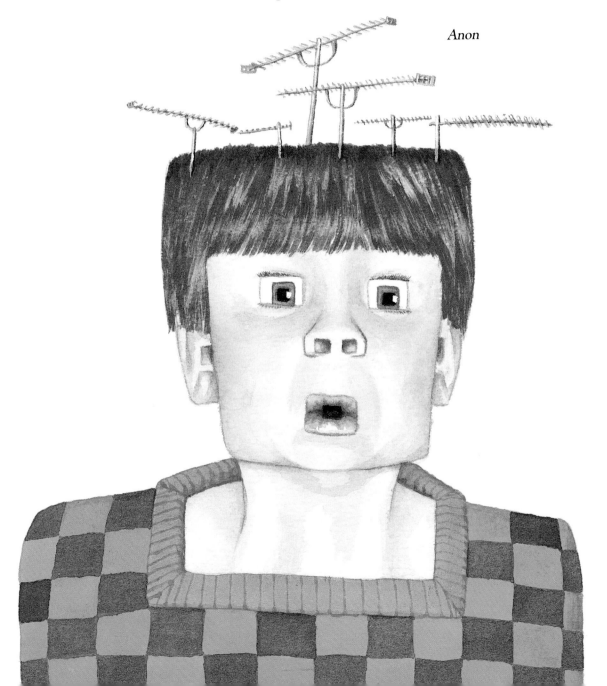

There was a young man dressed in
    black
Who went for a race in a sack,
But his grandmother said
He was better in bed
So she caught him and carried him
    back.

There was a small girl dressed in white
Who said she'd sit up the whole night,
But a mouse in the clock
Went a tick-a-tack-tock
And she ran off to bed in a fright.

Florence Harrison

LITTLE BOY'S PRAYER

Help me do the things I should,
Help me to be kind and good,
Doing no-one any hurt . . .
And make me soon grow out of my shirt.

Translated from the German by Rose Fyleman

TEARS

If all the little children who are crying at
  this minute
Could only see each other — they would all
  forget to cry.
I think they'd see how many children's tears
  the world has in it.
And wonder there were handkerchiefs enough
  to make them dry.

Marion St. John Webb

BOY

Such a scowling and a growling,
howling, yowling for a toy,
You grubby, snubby, tubby,
chubby, scrubby, little boy.

Hugh Lofting

TUBBING

Uncle Harry, hear the glee
Coming from the nursery!
Shall we just pop in to see
    Thomas in his tub?

In a soapy pond of joy,
Water as his only toy,
Sits my golden sailor-boy
    Thomas in his tub.

There he is, the little sweet,
Clutching at his rosy feet!
Make your toes and kisses meet,
    Thomas in the tub!

Partly come of fairy line,
Partly human, part divine,
How I love this rogue of mine,
    Thomas in the tub!

Norman Gale

THE PLUG-HOLE MAN

I know you're down there, Plug-hole Man,
   In the dark so utter,
For when I let the water out
   I hear you gasp and splutter.

And though I peer and peek and pry
   I've never seen you yet:
(I know you're down there, Plug-hole Man,
   In your home so wet).

But you will not be there for long
   For I've a *plan*, you see;
I'm going to catch you, Plug-hole Man,
   And Christian's helping me.

We'll fill the bath with water hot,
   Then give the plug a heave,
And rush down to the outside drain —
   And *catch* you as you leave!

Carey Blyton

17

SUSANNAH

Susannah put her apron on,
"I'm a witch, I'm a witch," she said,
"And if you don't give me some diamonds,
I'll magic you into brown bread.
Who am I?" she asked her teddy.
"You're a witch," her teddy bear said.

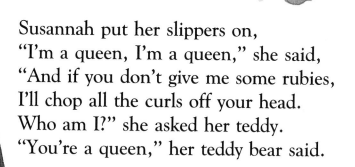

Susannah put her slippers on,
"I'm a queen, I'm a queen," she said,
"And if you don't give me some rubies,
I'll chop all the curls off your head.
Who am I?" she asked her teddy.
"You're a queen," her teddy bear said.

Susannah put her nightdress on,
"I'm so tired, so tired," she said.
Then she yawned and took out her ribbons
And snuggled down into her bed.
"Who am I?" she asked her teddy.
"Susannah," her teddy bear said.

Richard Edwards

LULLABY

Go to sleep my Teddy Bear.
Close your little button eyes,
And let me smooth your hair.
It feels so soft and silky that,
I'd love to cuddle down by you,
So,
Go to sleep, my darling Teddy Bear.

Anon

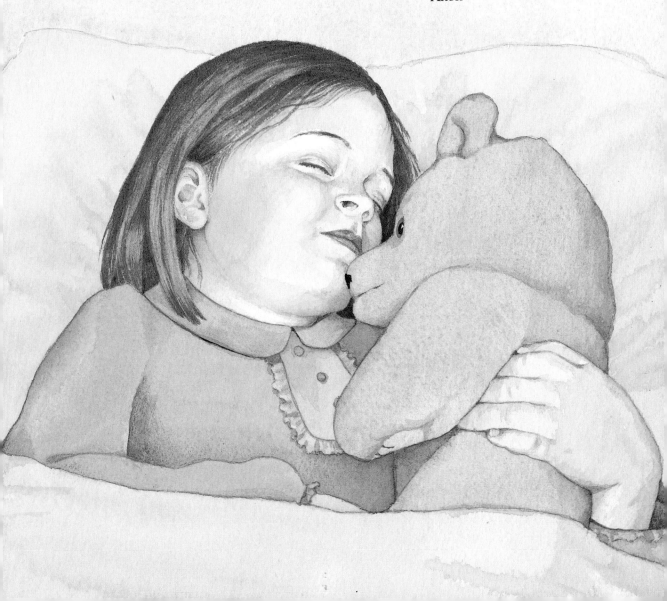

TOO TIRED

The tortoise that rang a bell
Somewhere inside its shell
As you pulled it along
And the lamb that turned
Its head from side to side
Stand in the back of a truck
As if they were tired of walking
And waited for a ride.

The dolls have stopped talking
And close their eyes in a cot,
The Teddy Bear lies sprawled out
With his ribbon untied
In the corner of a box.

The ducks are out of the water
And perch on the window ledge;
Among the books on the shelf
The rabbit is wedged
In a burrow all to himself.

Time to draw the curtains
And close the dolls' house door;
I and the toys are too tired
To play a minute more.

Stanley Cook

Good night, sleep tight,
 Don't let the bugs bite;
If they do, don't squall,
 Take a spoon and eat them all.

Anon

Good night and sweet repose,
 I hope the fleas will bite your nose;
And every bug as big as a bee
 And then you'll have good company.

Anon

Good night, sweet repose;
  Half the bed and all the clothes.

Anon

THE SWING

The garden-swing at the lawn's edge
Is hung beneath the hawthorn-hedge;
White branches droop above, and shed
Their petals on the swinger's head.
Here, now the day is almost done,
And leaves are pierced by the last sun,
I sit where hawthorn-breezes creep
Round me, and swing the hours to sleep:
Swinging alone —
By myself alone —
Alone,
Alone,
Alone.

In a soft shower the hawthorn-flakes descend.
Dusk falls at last. The dark-leaved branches bend
Earthward . . . The longest dream must have an end.

Now in my bedroom half-undressed,
My face against the window pressed,
I see once more the things which day
Gave me, and darkness takes away:
The garden-path still dimly white,
The lawn, the flower-beds sunk in night,
And, brushed by some uncertain breeze,
A ghostly swing beneath ghostly trees:
Swinging alone —
By itself alone —
Alone,
Alone,
Alone.

John Walsh

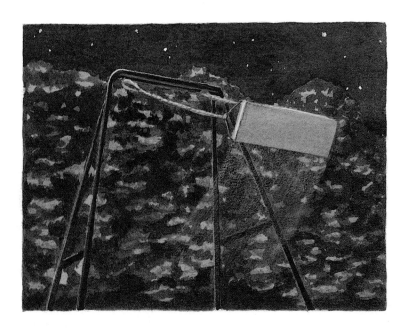

I know a dragon dark and green –
He's quite the handsomest I've seen –
Who (sometimes less and sometimes more)
Lives just behind my bedroom door.

And (sometimes less but often more)
That dragon just behind the door
Rolls one eye up and one eye down
And turns into my dressing gown.

He doesn't do it in the night,
But in the early morning light
Where dragon was, there on its hook
That dressing gown gives me a look.

I've asked the dragon if he'd stay
And be a dragon through the day
But with a smile and with a frown
He turns into a dressing gown.

Russell Hoban

FINGUMMY . . .

Fingummy's fat
And Fingummy's small,
And Fingummy lives
With the boots in the hall.

If Fingummy bites,
If Fingummy tears,
If Fingummy chases you
Up the stairs

Shout "Bumble-Bee Soup
And Bluebottle Jam."
And run up to bed as fast as you can!

'Cos Fingummy lives
Where there's never no light
And Fingummy makes
The dark sounds of the night,
And Fingummy's fat
And Fingummy's small
And Fingummy lives
In the dark, in the hall . . .

Mike Harding

27

THE SOUNDS IN THE EVENING

The sounds in the evening
Go all through the house,
The click of the clock
And the pick of the mouse,
The footsteps of people
Upon the top floor,
The skirts of my mother
That brush by my door,
The crick in the boards,
And the creak of the chairs,
The fluttering murmurs
Outside on the stairs,
The ring at the bell,
The arrival of guests,
The laugh of my father
At one of his jests,

The clashing of dishes
As dinner goes in,
The babble of voices
That distance makes thin,
The mewings of cats
That seem just by my ear,
The hooting of owls
That can never seem near,

The queer little noises
That no one explains —
Till the moon through the slats
Of my window-blind rains,
And the world of my eyes
And my ears melts like steam
As I find in my pillow
The world of my dream.

Eleanor Farjeon

ALL ON MY OWN

The night-wind rattles the window-frame —
I wake up shivering, shivering, all alone.
Darkness. Silence. What's the time?
Mother's asleep, and Dad's not home.
Shivering in the corner, shivering all alone.

Who's there? — standing behind the curtain?
Shivering in the corner, no need to cry . . .
It's only the shadow of the tree in the garden
Shaking and sighing as the wind rushes by.
Shivering in the corner, and no need to cry.

Brian Lee

LATE-NIGHT CALLER

The tick of the clock,
the click of the lock,
a shoeless sock
on the stair,

the groan of the floor,
the squeak of a door,
the sigh of a drawer —
who's there?

A current of air,
a pencil of light —
"I'm back, son. All right?
Goodnight!"

Sue Cowling

FULL MOON

One night as Dick lay half asleep,
   Into his drowsy eyes
A great still light began to creep
   From out the silent skies.
It was the lovely moon's, for when
   He raised his dreamy head,
Her surge of silver filled the pane
   And streamed across his bed.
So, for a while, each gazed at each —
   Dick and the solemn moon —
Till, climbing slowly on her way,
   She vanished, and was gone.

Walter de la Mare

ABOVE THE DOCK

Above the quiet dock in midnight,
Tangled in the tall mast's corded height,
Hangs the moon. What seemed so far away
Is but a child's balloon, forgotten after play.

T. E. Hulme

THE GREAT BROWN OWL

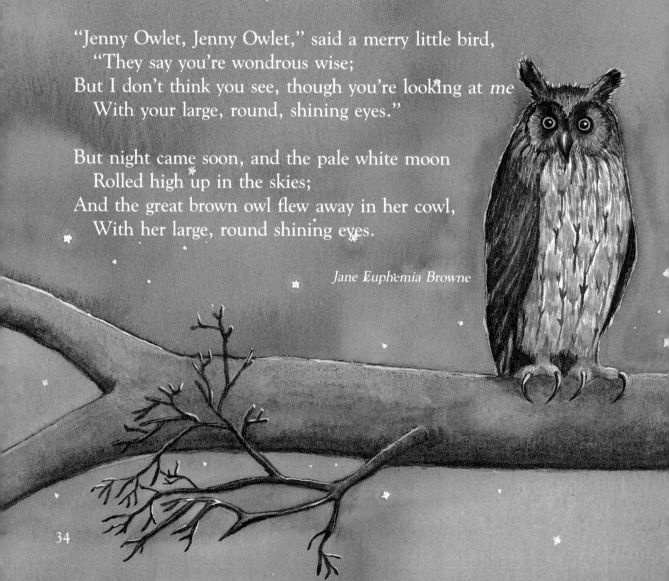

The brown owl sits in the ivy bush,
  And she looketh wondrous wise,
With a horny beak beneath her cowl,
  And a pair of large round eyes.

She sat all day on the selfsame spray,
  From sunrise till sunset;
And the dim, grey light it was all too bright
  For the owl to see in yet.

"Jenny Owlet, Jenny Owlet," said a merry little bird,
  "They say you're wondrous wise;
But I don't think you see, though you're looking at *me*
  With your large, round, shining eyes."

But night came soon, and the pale white moon
  Rolled high up in the skies;
And the great brown owl flew away in her cowl,
  With her large, round shining eyes.

Jane Euphemia Browne

THAT'S WHAT WE'D DO

If you were an owl,
   And I were an owl,
And this were a tree,
   And the moon came out,
I know what we'd do.
We would stand, we two,
On a bough of the tree;
You'd wink at me,
And I'd wink at you;
That's what we'd do,
   Beyond a doubt.

I'd give you a rose
For your lovely nose,
And you'd look at me
   Without turning about.
I know what we'd do
(That is, I and you);
Why, you'd sing to me,
And I'd sing to you;
That's what we'd do,
   When the moon came out.

Mary Mapes Dodge

35

ONE O'CLOCK

One of the clock, and silence deep
Then up the stairway black and steep
The old house-cat comes creepy-creep
With soft feet goes from room to room
Her green eyes shining through the gloom,
   And finds all fast asleep.

Katharine Pyle

HICKORY, DICKORY, DOCK

Hickory, Dickory, Dock,
The mouse ran down the clock —
She had watched the cat go out of the door,
She saw some crumbs on the kitchen floor,
And she gobbled them up — Tick-tock!

Hickory, Dickory, Dock,
The mouse ran up the clock —
For she heard the stealthy tread of the cat,
And she didn't care to stay after that,
So she scampered back — Tick-tock!

Hickory, Dickory, Dock,
The mouse slept in the clock —
But when she awoke, she gnawed her way
Through the old clock-case one winter day,
And never came back — Tick-tock!

Anon

NO HICKORY NO DICKORY NO DOCK

Wasn't me
Wasn't me
said the little mouse
I didn't run up no clock

You could hickory me
You could dickory me
or lock me in a dock

I still say
I didn't run up no clock

Was me who ran under your bed
Was me who bit into your bread
Was me who nibbled your cheese

But please please
I didn't run up no clock
no hickory
no dickory
no dock.

John Agard

THE HAPPY HEDGEHOG

The happiness of hedgehogs
Lies in complete repose.
They spend the months of winter
In a long delicious doze;
And if they note the time at all
They think "How fast it goes!"

E. V. Rieu

Lullaby, oh, lullaby!
Flowers are closed and lambs are sleeping;
   Lullaby, oh, lullaby!
Stars are up, the moon is peeping;
   Lullaby, oh, lullaby!
While the birds are silence keeping,
   (Lullaby, oh, lullaby!)
Sleep, my baby, fall a-sleeping,
   Lullaby, oh, lullaby!

Christina Rossetti

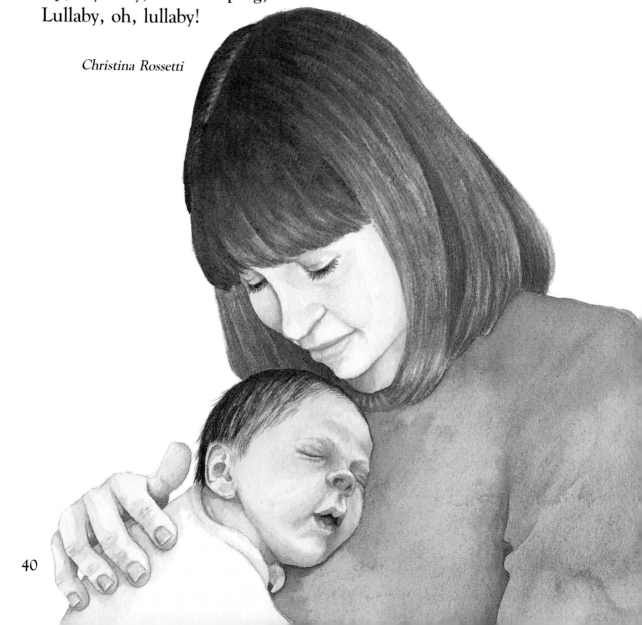

THE COTTAGER TO HER INFANT

The days are cold, the nights are long,
The Northwind sings a doleful song;
Then hush again upon my breast;
All merry things are now at rest,
   Save thee, my pretty love!

The kitten sleeps upon the hearth;
The crickets long have ceased their mirth;
There's nothing stirring in the house
Save one wee, hungry, nibbling mouse,
   Then why so busy thou?

Nay! start not at the sparkling light;
'Tis but the moon that shines so bright
On the window-pane bedropped with rain:
There, little darling! sleep again,
   And wake when it is day.

Dorothy Wordsworth

By the shores of Gitche Gumee,
By the shining Big-Sea-Water,
Stood the wigwam of Nokomis,
Daughter of the Moon, Nokomis.
Dark behind it rose the forest,
Rose the black and gloomy
    pine-trees,
Rose the firs with cones upon them;
Bright before it beat the water,
Beat the clear and sunny water,
Beat the shining Big-Sea-Water.
There the wrinkled, old Nokomis
Nursed the little Hiawatha,
Rocked him in his linden cradle,
Bedded soft in moss and rushes,
Safely bound with reindeer sinews;
Stilled his fretful wail by saying,
"Hush! the Naked Bear will hear
thee!"
Lulled him into slumber, singing,
"Ewa-yea! my little owlet!
Who is this, that lights the wigwam?
With his great eyes lights the
    wigwam?
Ewa-yea! my little owlet!"

From HIAWATHA'S CHILDHOOD, *Longfellow*

THE GREEN TRAIN

The Blue train for the South – but the Green Train for us.
Nobody knows when the Green Train departs.
Nobody sees her off. There is no noise; no fuss;
No luggage on the Green Train;
No whistle when she starts.
But quietly at the right time they wave the green light
And she slides past the platform and plunges into the night.

Wonderful people walking down the long Green Train,
As the engine gathers speed.
And voices talking.
"Where does she go to, Guard?"
Where indeed?
But what does it matter
So long as the night is starred?
Who cares for time, and who cares for the place,
So long as the Green Train thunders on into space?

E. V. Rieu

NIGHT IS . . .

headlights switching on in cars
in the thickening dark,
children shouted in from play
emptying the park:

lights flicked on in bedrooms,
street lamps suddenly humming,
curtains being swished across,
the Sandman's coming!

putting fresh pyjamas on,
tucking in the sheet,
stories from a story book,
hot-water-bottle feet!

head upon the pillow
trying to settle down:
what's that moving on the door?
just a dressing gown!

rubbing itchy eyeballs,
hugging Teddy Bear,
Want a Drink of Water!
Mummy Someone's There!

turning over on your side,
pretending not to peep,
gone before you know it
deep-down into sleep.

Matt Simpson

Here we are all, by day; by night we are hurled
By dreams, each one into a several world.

Robert Herrick

ACKNOWLEDGEMENTS

The editor and publishers are grateful to the following copyright holders for permission to include copyright material in this anthology:

JOHN AGARD, 'No Hickory No Dickory No Dock' from *No Hickory No Dickory No Dock*, Viking 1991; to the author and Caroline Sheldon Literary Agency.

CAREY BLYTON, 'The Plug-hole Man' from *Bananas in Pyjamas;* to the author and the Australian Broadcasting Corporation.

STANLEY COOK, 'Too Tired' from *Dragon on the Wall* © Stanley Cook, 1992, first published by Blackie Children's Books.

SUE COWLING, 'Late Night Caller' from *What is a Kumquat?;* to the author and Faber and Faber Ltd.

WALTER DE LA MARE, 'Full Moon'; to The Literary Trustees of Walter de la Mare and The Society of Authors as their representative.

RICHARD EDWARDS, 'Susannah' from *The Word Party,* Lutterworth Press; to the author.

ELEANOR FARJEON, 'Bedtime' and 'The Sounds in the Evening' from *Silver Sand and Snow,* Michael Joseph; to Gervase Farjeon as Literary Executor of the Eleanor Farjeon Estate.

ROSE FYLEMAN, (translator), 'Little Boy's Prayer' from *Over the Treetops;* to The Society of Authors as the literary representative of the Estate of Rose Fyleman.

MIKE HARDING, 'Fingummy'; to the author.

RUSSELL HOBAN, 'Dragon into Dressing Gown'; to the author.

BRIAN LEE, 'All on my own'; to the author.

JAMES REEVES, 'Time to go home' © James Reeves from *The Wandering Moon and other Poems,* Puffin Books. Reprinted by permission of the James Reeves Estate.

E. V. RIEU, 'The Happy Hedgehog' and 'The Green Train' from *Cuckoo Calling,* Methuen 1933; to E. V. Rieu's children.

MATT SIMPSON, 'Night is . . .'; to the author.

JOHN WALSH, 'The Swing' from *Poets in Hand,* Puffin books; to Mrs A. M. Walsh.

The editor and publishers have made every effort to trace the holders of copyright in all poems included in this anthology. If, however, any query should arise, it should be addressed to the publishers.

INDEX OF POETS, TITLES, AND FIRST LINES